# Disney

# Tangled

## The Essential Guide

**DK**

*Rapunzel and Flynn swing into action and adventure*

# Disney

# Tangled

## The Essential Guide

Written by
Barbara Bazaldua

# Contents

# Once upon a time...

...a magical flower grew from a drop of golden sunlight. Mother Gothel, a vain and selfish woman, guarded the Golden Flower and used its power to keep herself young. One day, in a nearby kingdom, the Queen announced that she was to have a baby. But the Queen became ill. The people of her kingdom found and uprooted the flower. They made it into a soup, and it healed the Queen. She gave birth to a baby girl with golden hair that held the blossom's healing power. To mark the birth, the King and Queen launched a floating lantern. But all too soon a vengeful Mother Gothel stole the baby and hid her in a tower so she could use the magical hair. Little did the evil woman know that not even the walls of a tower can contain the spirit of a true princess...

# Rapunzel

**R**apunzel may have lived her whole life locked inside a secret tower, but that hasn't made her shy. Energetic, curious, and creative, she has a bold spirit and the courage to take her destiny into her own hands!

## Magical Hair

Rapunzel's hair isn't just long and beautiful. It is magical, too! When Rapunzel or Mother Gothel sing a special song, Rapunzel's hair glows and heals anyone touching it.

*Rapunzel's hair is strong! She often hangs from it to paint on the tower walls*

*A hairbrush is Rapunzel's most important grooming accessory*

*Lavender is Rapunzel's favorite color*

*Simple dresses suit Rapunzel's lifestyle*

## Misleading Mother

Mother Gothel is the only "mother" Rapunzel can remember. When she tells Rapunzel frightening stories about the outside world, Rapunzel believes her.

Rapunzel finds living in the tower can be hard work! She does every chore in the tower and has to pull Mother Gothel up to the window with her hair.

## Likes...

• Watching the beautiful floating lanterns.

• Getting creative.

• Chatting with—or at—her friend Pascal.

*Rapunzel is a born dreamer*

## ...and Dislikes

• Too many tangles!

• Mother Gothel telling her that she is weak.

• Never feeling the grass beneath her feet.

## Floating Lights

Every year on her birthday, Rapunzel sees floating lights from her window. She feels as if they are meant for her. She doesn't know it yet, but she's right! Rapunzel longs to go outside and watch them.

# Mother Gothel

Mother Gothel is the only mother Rapunzel has ever known, but the vain, self-centered woman does not have a drop of motherly affection in her heart. Mother Gothel says she loves Rapunzel, but all she truly cares about is the teenager's magical hair.

*Mother Gothel is obsessed with having youthful skin and hair*

## "Rapunzel, let down your hair!"

### Control Freak

A mistress of manipulation, Mother Gothel intimidates and bullies Rapunzel with subtle put-downs, guilt trips, and mean-spirited teasing. She scares Rapunzel with tall tales about the "ruffians" in the outside world to make sure Rapunzel doesn't try to leave.

*Mother Gothel chooses flowing styles to flatter her figure*

### Magic Flower

Mother Gothel used the magical Golden Flower to stay youthful before the magic transferred to Rapunzel's hair and she began using that instead.

# Likes and Dislikes

- Admiring her youthful face in the mirror.

- Stroking Rapunzel's hair.

- Manipulating Rapunzel.

- Growing old.

- Being asked about the floating lights.

- Not getting her way.

## Hair-raising Climb

While Rapunzel is trapped in the tower, Mother Gothel comes and goes as she pleases. When Mother Gothel calls, "Let down your hair," Rapunzel loops her hair around a pulley system to pull Mother Gothel up. Mother Gothel doesn't do a thing except complain that Rapunzel takes too long.

## Did you know?

Mother Gothel is actually centuries old. But she doesn't look a day over forty thanks to Rapunzel's magical hair.

## Plant Craft

Mother Gothel is skilled at gathering wild plants for beauty. Mother Gothel makes a fern seed face mask for her skin and drinks dragonmint tea to freshen her breath.

## Hidden Tower

With such impassable terrain around it and with Rapunzel's bedroom being so high up, the tower was the perfect place for Mother Gothel to hide Rapunzel.

*This is the window from which Rapunzel lets down her hair.*

*Was the tower built by men or magic? No one really knows!*

## Towering Facts

➤ The tower is 95 feet (30 meters) tall.

➤ Rapunzel's bedroom is in the loft of the tower above Mother Gothel's bedroom.

➤ The tower is situated in a box canyon with a tall waterfall that tumbles into the midst.

# The Tower

**M**other Gothel's secret tower stands in the middle of a mysterious valley surrounded by mountains and forest. Only Mother Gothel knows about a secret staircase that leads to the base of the tower where there is a sealed-off door hidden behind ivy.

## Living Space

The tower has a spacious central room, with a large fireplace, high ceilings, a kitchen, and balconies. There is space for a large wardrobe, Mother Gothel's mirror, and for Rapunzel to do her hobbies and stretches.

## Secret Staircase

Hidden by a trapdoor in the tower floor, the secret staircase leads to the world outside. The entrance was closed off once Rapunzel's hair grew long enough to pull Mother Gothel up to the top of the tower.

*The tower is built on lush vegetation where Mother Gothel can harvest plants and herbs*

# Mommy Dearest

**W**ith a parent like Mother Gothel, who needs enemies? The vain villainess quickly flits between faked fondness and nasty needling. When Rapunzel tries to stand up to her, Mother Gothel's maternal mask comes off and her true personality is revealed: It is not pretty.

*Mother Gothel's hug is more menacing than motherly*

## "Don't ever ask to leave the tower again."

### Trust Your Mother

Mother Gothel could write a book about being devious. First she uses scare tactics. Then she uses emotional blackmail to make Rapunzel feel sorry for her. She is a very scheming lady.

*Mother Gothel will never release Rapunzel*

### Did you know?

Mother Gothel needs daily "doses" of the magic in Rapunzel's long locks to keep her from growing old. She's hanging onto her youthful looks by a hair!

## Just Teasing

To make Rapunzel believe she needs the protection of the tower, Mother Gothel does everything she can to destroy the teen's confidence by viciously suggesting she is careless, weak, childish, and ditzy. She tells Rapunzel she is only saying this for her own good, of course.

## Tall Tales

Mother Gothel keeps Rapunzel frightened of the outside world with a long list of gruesome things including huge insects, ruffians, deadly plants, thugs, diseases, and worst of all, men with pointy teeth!

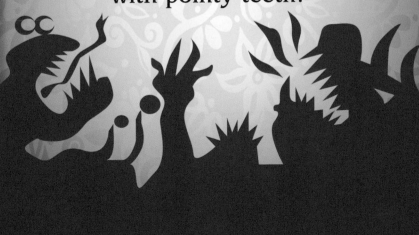

## Shut Down

Mother Gothel shows her true colors when Rapunzel says she wants to see the floating lights for her birthday. She slams the shutters closed and in the shadowy darkness proceeds to terrify Rapunzel with tales of the dangers outside.

# Flynn Rider

Raised in an orphanage, petty criminal Flynn dreamed of becoming a swashbuckling hero like the ones he read about in his favorite childhood book. Independent Flynn always looks out for number one first. But when he meets Rapunzel, his attitude begins to change.

*Flynn is very handsome and he knows it*

## Greed is Good

Flynn hopes that stealing a crown from the royal family will allow him to live a life of ease and riches because that is what he thinks he wants.

*Flynn relies on his sharp wit rather than any weapons*

## Bad Guy Image

Flynn prides himself on looking good—even when he is acting badly. He doesn't mind being a wanted man; he just wishes they could make him look right. There is no way his nose is *that* big!

*Good strong boots for fast getaways, narrow escapes, and climbing towers*

# Likes and Dislikes

- Getting away with it.

- Swashbuckling adventures.

- Practising his "handsome" look.

- Making Rapunzel smile.

- His real name— Eugene Fitzherbert.

- Frying pans.

- Stubborn horses.

- Falling off cliffs.

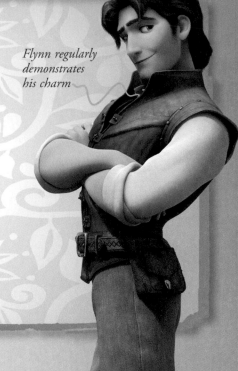

*Flynn regularly demonstrates his charm*

## Dangerous Company

Flynn works with the criminal Stabbington brothers to snatch the crown, but he outsmarts and ditches the gruesome twosome as soon as he can. He prefers solo swashbuckling.

## Lucky Discovery

On the run, Flynn navigates his way through a dense forest. He comes to an opening that houses a tall tower. It is going to be a high climb, but Flynn believes this could be the perfect hiding place.

## Did you know?

Flynn's favorite book is *The Tales of Flynnegan Rider*, about a swashbuckling rogue. Flynn read it as a youngster, adopted the name, and tried to live up to the lifestyle.

# Pascal

Spunky chameleon Pascal is Rapunzel's best friend. He is her confidante, coach, and cheerleader. He encourages her in her plan to go see the floating lights. Supportive and caring, the loyal lizard sticks by Rapunzel and helps her discover who she really is.

## Colorful Friend

Although Pascal doesn't speak, he communicates clearly through his facial expressions and body language. He also shows how he is feeling by changing color.

*Pascal's eyes swivel so he can see everything*

*Pascal's long tail helps him balance and hang from things*

*Pascal is a true blue friend, even when he's green*

*Feet that can cling on to wa... are great for climbing*

## Wake-up Call

Pascal is always quick-thinking. After Rapunzel whacks Flynn with a skillet, he is out like a light. Pascal manages to wake the swashbuckling rogue up fast: A quick flick of the tongue does the trick.

Pascal is always happy to lend Rapunzel a helping foot with her daily chores. In fact, he never ever leaves her side.

# Mood Swinging

Pascal changes color to fit his mood or surroundings.

**Blue**
• Sad or frightened

**Red**
• Bashful or angry

**Yellow**
• Near Rapunzel's hair

## You Can Do It

Pascal always hides from scary Mother Gothel, but he feels the need to come out of the woodwork when Flynn arrives. He encourages Rapunzel to be tough with the intruder.

# Rapunzel's Hobbies

Rapunzel has lived in the tower for nearly eighteen years—that's about 200 months, or 900 weeks, or 6,500 days! She is very creative and resourceful so she manages to stay busy with a variety of hobbies and activities.

### Knitting
Rapunzel finds knitting very relaxing. She has created so many beautiful scarves for herself and Pascal, she has lost count.

### Pottery
Rapunzel enjoys doing pottery, but how many pots does one girl need? Besides, Pascal thinks this hobby is a little too sticky.

### Baking
Rapunzel loves the scent of freshly baked bread and cookies. Her pies are super delicious. Pascal likes this hobby best.

### Rock 'n' Roll
Rapunzel has never heard a real orchestra or musical group, but that hasn't stopped her from teaching herself how to make music.

### Dressmaking
Rapunzel loves to dress up. Or she would if she had more than one dress! Instead, she makes clothes for Pascal—who is not always happy with the result.

## Puzzling

On a sunny day, Rapunzel likes to lie on the floor in the sun and work on a jigsaw puzzle. Ever-helpful Pascal is good at finding pieces for her.

**"It's not so bad in there."**

## Painting

Rapunzel is a talented artist. Her favorite things to paint are the beautiful floating lights that she loves to watch from her tower window.

*Rapunzel has a large collection of brushes—for both hair and paint!*

## Mural

Rapunzel's best painting is the giant mural that she adds to constantly. She can always find space for more floating lights or birds.

*Rapunzel is very careful not to get her dress dirty when she's painting*

## Darts

Pascal is too little to throw darts but he nudges Rapunzel to make sure she hits her target every time.

# All Tied Up

**W**hen Flynn climbs up into Rapunzel's tower, he thinks it is a great place to hide from the Stabbingtons, the royal guards, and their horse Maximus. But he's wrong!

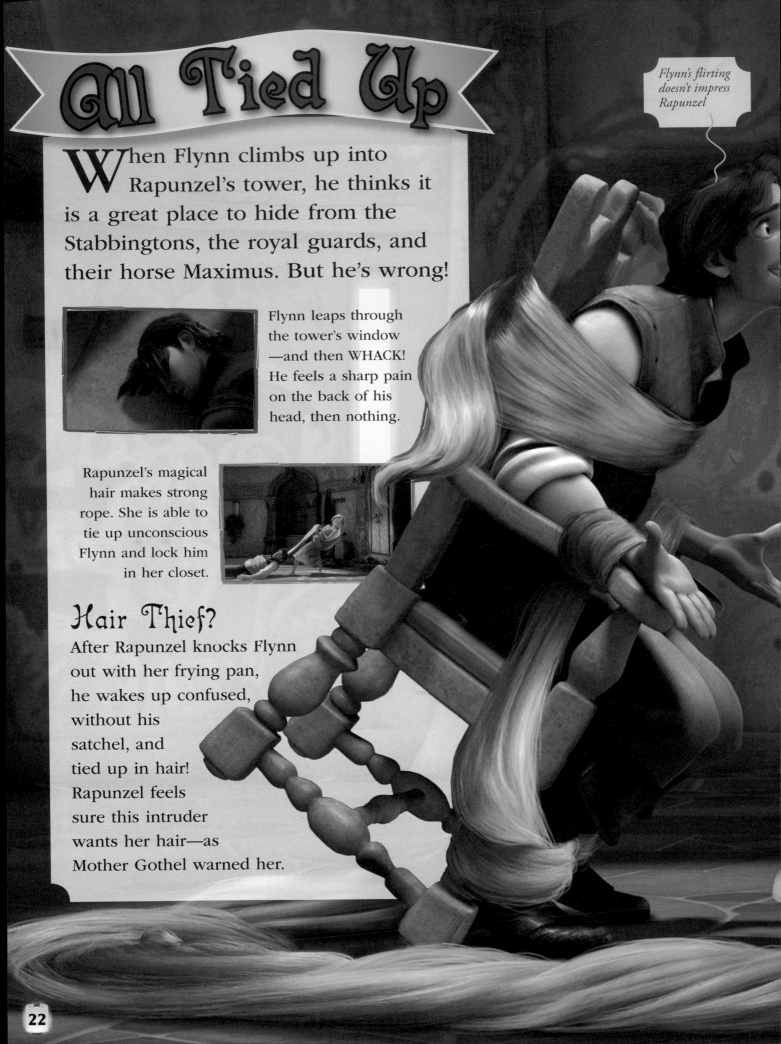

Flynn leaps through the tower's window —and then WHACK! He feels a sharp pain on the back of his head, then nothing.

Rapunzel's magical hair makes strong rope. She is able to tie up unconscious Flynn and lock him in her closet.

## Hair Thief?

After Rapunzel knocks Flynn out with her frying pan, he wakes up confused, without his satchel, and tied up in hair! Rapunzel feels sure this intruder wants her hair—as Mother Gothel warned her.

*Rapunzel is determined to get her own way*

## "Is this... hair?"

Flynn flashes his best "handsome" look, but Rapunzel is not affected.

Rapunzel decides to trust Flynn. His teeth aren't pointy—but she still keeps her frying pan handy!

## Deals and Promises

Rapunzel tells Flynn her deal. She will return his satchel if he guides her to see the lights. Flynn can trust Rapunzel—when she makes a promise, she never, ever breaks it.

# Maximus

**M**aximus is part of the royal guard and takes his duties seriously. Strong and fast, Max is a tough horse who doesn't give up easily. He is frustrated by Flynn—his toughest rival so far—but that makes him more determined to catch his man.

## Brains and Brawn

Max is more than just an enormous mass of fast-moving muscle. Wily Max isn't easy to outsmart. Just ask Flynn, who tried and failed.

## Loyal Steed

Maximus comes from a long line of horses who have proudly served the royal guard. He has the stern bearing and strict discipline of a true soldier. He prides himself on carrying out orders, whatever it takes.

*Maximus' chestplate shows he is a palace horse*

Max shows his tracking skills when he is looking for Flynn. He sniffs at the ground like a dog. Escaping Max is much harder than Flynn expects.

Maximus and Flynn are well-matched adversaries. Flynn is a smart daredevil and Maximus eats danger for breakfast. They could never imagine that they will end up being friends.

## Likes and Dislikes

*Maximus can't hide his feelings*

- Getting his man.
- Appreciation.
- Having his muzzle nuzzled.
- Fresh apples.
- Rapunzel.

- Being told off.
- Falling off cliffs.
- Being outwitted.
- Wormy apples.
- Flynn.

*Max's saddlebags carry important supplies, like apples*

*Max is 66 inches (168 cm) high, which is 16.2 hands in "horse speak"*

### Did you know?

Maximus is an Andalusian breed of horse. His ancestors were ridden in battles and are famous for strength and bravery–just like Maximus!

### Big Softie

Maximus acts tough, but he is really a big softie inside. He is a pushover for Rapunzel's calming voice and kind words. Horses love sugar, so it's no wonder Max falls for Rapunzel's sweet-talking.

## Great Escape

"Rapunzel, let down your hair!" Rapunzel has lowered her locks thousands of times for Mother Gothel. Now, for the first time, she's doing it for herself—so she can finally see the floating lights she loves so much.

# Free At Last

When Mother Gothel tells Rapunzel she will never leave the tower, the determined lass decides to take matters into her own hair. But she needs a guide to see the lights. It is lucky for her that Flynn just happened to appear when he did.

## The Long Way Down

Rapunzel knows the best way to get to the bottom of the tower—abseiling down her hair! Flynn's arrows are no comparison for her speedy descent.

Rapunzel is a natural at abseiling as she glides effortlessly to the ground.

## Swinging

Finally on solid ground, Rapunzel feels guilty about disobeying her mother, but she also rejoices in her freedom. This is her best day ever!

*Pascal loves watching Rapunzel so happy*

*Rapunzel uses her hair to get into the swing of things*

A rustle in the bushes scares Rapunzel. Is it a thug with pointy teeth? No—just a cute bunny!

## Impatient Flynn

Flynn is fascinated by Rapunzel but he still doesn't want to be her guide. While she plays around, the scheming swashbuckler tries to think of a way to disentangle himself from her.

Rapunzel has often wondered how grass feels. Now, she knows—it's fabulous!

# The Stabbingtons

The Stabbingtons are identical twin brothers who share their brutish looks and temperament. One word best describes the Stabbington brothers: mean. So mean, they don't even have first names. Everyone knows who they are. They may not be bright, but they're as strong and stubborn as oxen.

## Life of crime

The Stabbingtons' path of crime started the moment they could walk. Before they were three they had:

☠ Looted the local bakery.

☠ Terrorized the neighbor's watch dog by biting its tail.

☠ Crashed the family horse and wagon on a high-speed chase.

☠ Started shaving—with stolen daggers!

Flynn teamed up with the bad brothers because he needed their muscle to nab the crown. He soon regrets it and leaves their wicked company.

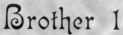

# Brother 1

The first brother is strong, fast, fearless, and dangerous as a coiled snake. His only weakness? He's all brawn and no brain. The only noticeable difference between him and his brother is the eye patch. He secretly quite likes looking a bit different from his brother.

# Brother 2

The thick-skulled and ham-fisted second brother makes other bad guys look good—not that they would hang around long enough to find out.

# Double Dealer

When Rapunzel escapes the tower, Mother Gothel makes a pact with the Stabbington brothers to help them get revenge on Flynn. The brothers agree, not knowing that the double-dealing diva stops at nothing to get what she wants.

# The Snuggly Duckling

The name is the only cute thing about this pub. The inn may look quaint on the outside, but inside it reeks of dirty dishes, dirty socks, and as Flynn says "really bad man smell." When Flynn takes Rapunzel to The Snuggly Duckling, he doesn't tell her it's a hangout for thugs and ruffians.

## Frosty Reception

The pub's regular visitors are not keen on new arrivals at their favorite haunt. They can be quite intimidating when they want to be. Rapunzel experiences their hostility firsthand when she arrives there—but the place soon falls into song and laughter.

## Hidden Pub

The Snuggly Ducking is not easy to find. Buried deep in a forest, it only attracts the toughest types.

*The pub is in a very old building that has gradually curved with the tree next to it*

*Just the sight of the pub's sign is enough to send some people in the other direction*

*The trees around the pub are curled and gnarled because they are centuries old*

## Dish of the Day

The Snuggly Duckling's cook whips up meals out of anything he finds lying around. Luckily, the thugs and ruffians have cast iron stomachs! Is that a sock in the stew?

## Menu

Mystery Meatloaf

Lizard Stew

Cabbage Surprise

Black and Blue-berry Pie

# Pub Thugs

The thugs and ruffians at the Snuggly Duckling look as though they've stepped out of Rapunzel's worst nightmare. They're hairy and scary. But when Rapunzel inspires them to talk about their dreams, they each reveal a softer side. It just goes to prove you should never judge a thug by his looks.

*Atilla made this helmet himself*

Wanted
Atilla

## Atilla

Atilla's name strikes fear into the bravest hearts. But his sublime cupcakes strike hunger into everyone's tummies. He'd love to hang up his horned helmet and focus on beating eggs instead of people.

Wanted
Tor

## Tor

Inspired by Rapunzel, Tor reveals the little seed of a dream growing inside his hairy chest. He is tired of rearranging faces. He wants to be a florist and arrange blossoms instead.

Wanted
Shorty

## Shorty

Shorty is so close to the floor, it's hard to hear what he dreams about. Being taller? Having a growth spurt? Learning to walk on stilts? Or perhaps he's just happy as he is because he really has a good heart.

# Raucous Ruffians

After a long day of creating mayhem, the thugs and ruffians enjoy gathering at The Snuggly Duckling for a bite to eat and rowdy brawl or two. Even the roughest ruffians need to relax.

## Vladamir

Big, clumsy Vladamir is the last thug you would expect to collect delicate, dainty ceramic unicorns! He even gives one to Rapunzel as a farewell gift.

Wanted
Vladamir

Wanted
Big Nose

## Big Nose

Big Nose would love to be a poet. There are just a couple of things stopping him. He can't think of a rhyme for "thug" other than "ugh" and he has trouble just writing his own name.

## Hookhand

Hookhand dreams of being a concert pianist. His fingers are too big, but he certainly can hook an audience with the energy of his performance.

Wanted
Hookhand

*Shorty is much less aggressive than the other pub thugs*

## Authority

The captain of the palace guard doesn't fear the thugs or ruffians. He has the authority of the law behind him.

*Max likes nothing better than getting his nose dirty on a tracking mission*

# Escape

The pub thugs help Rapunzel and Flynn escape the Stabbingtons, royal guards, and Max. Rapunzel and Flynn both leap into a secret tunnel that leads to a deep, dark cavern. This is a true test of their spirit—and Max's tracking skills.

## Rising Water

Flynn's lantern goes out when the cavern begins to flood. He and Rapunzel are able to escape only when Rapunzel reveals she has magical hair. Its glow helps them to find their way out.

## Maximus Gives In

Maximus eventually finds Flynn and tries to nab him. But Rapunzel shows she is a natural with animals, despite only ever having met one before. She charms the stubborn steed into letting Flynn go free—at least for the day.

## Healing Hair

After Flynn injures his hand in the dark cavern, Rapunzel uses her magical hair to heal it. Flynn finally discovers that she has never left the tower before today and the reason why.

## Family Ties

When Mother Gothel surprises Rapunzel outside the cavern, Rapunzel reveals she thinks Flynn likes her. Mother Gothel is furious and cunningly plants seeds of doubt about whether Flynn's loyalty lies with Rapunzel or the stolen crown.

# Hairdos... and Don'ts

**W**hen your hair is as long as Rapunzel's, it needs extra special care. She has learned some important hair care tips. After all, with those long locks, one little mistake can easily become a hair-raising mess!

## Do...

... braid your hair to keep it off the ground. This is very important if you're going out and don't want people stepping on it. That's a real drag. Besides, a braid is really pretty!

*Pascal is always a willing assistant when Rapunzel needs some help with her long tresses*

## Don't...

... let your hair down for anyone without proper safety precautions. Wrap it around a pulley first to avoid too much discomfort when they climb it.

# Don't...

... forget to condition your hair. This will keep it strong, which is essential if you often swing from it.

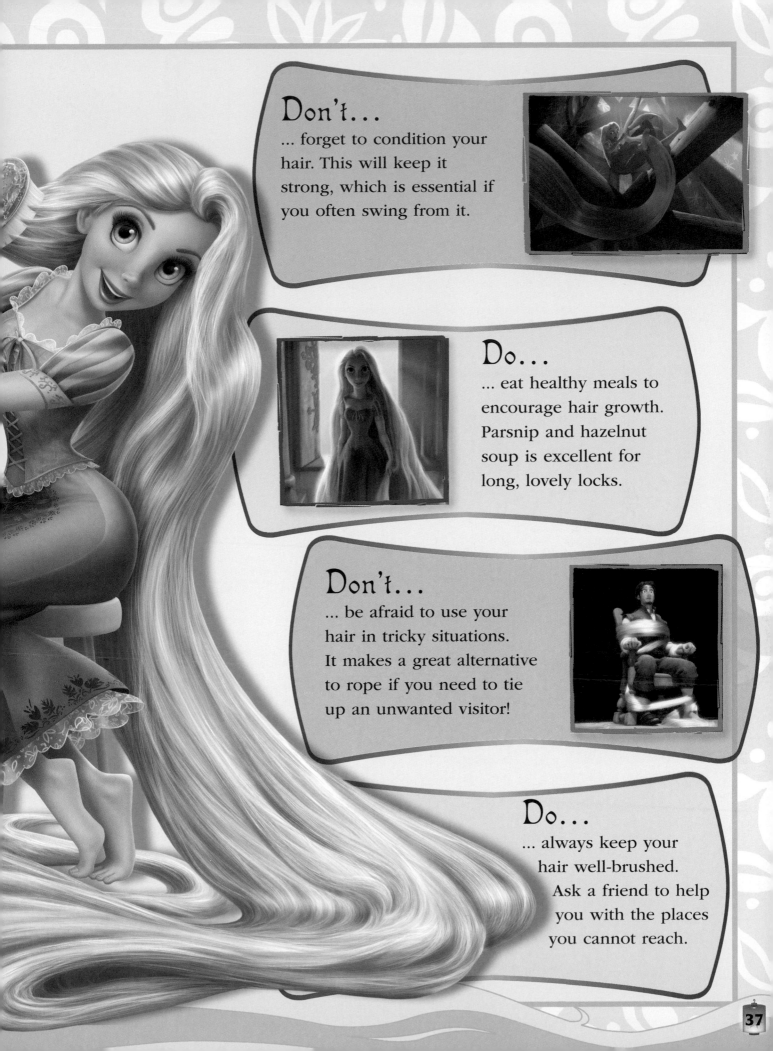

# Do...

... eat healthy meals to encourage hair growth. Parsnip and hazelnut soup is excellent for long, lovely locks.

# Don't...

... be afraid to use your hair in tricky situations. It makes a great alternative to rope if you need to tie up an unwanted visitor!

# Do...

... always keep your hair well-brushed. Ask a friend to help you with the places you cannot reach.

# Lovable Rogue

hough he is handsome, clever, and daring, Flynn Rider is a petty thief who lives by his wit and charm. Unlike the Stabbingtons, Flynn is not very bad—he just sometimes finds himself on the wrong side of the law.

## Daring Deeds

Cunning Flynn can usually get out of any tight spot with quick thinking and the following athletic skills:

• Ducking and dodging guards' speeding arrows.

• Climbing and clambering up walls.

• Swerving and speeding out of tight spots.

• Hiding, sneaking, and tricking.

## Wanted Man

Flynn's face adorns more trees in the forest than any other thief's. He is well known to all the royal guards and is recognized wherever he goes. Amazingly, he has never been caught!

**WANTED**

**DEAD or ALIVE**
Flynn Rider
THIEF

## Reformed Character

When Flynn meets Rapunzel, he begins to see the world through her eyes. He starts to change and realize it is best to see the good in people. He leaves his bad ways behind him. He always did hate WANTED posters!

# Kingdom

Eventually, Rapunzel and Flynn arrive in the kingdom on her eighteenth birthday. It is situated on an island and has quiet cobblestone streets, sparkling fountains, charming homes, and the stunning royal castle. Rapunzel loves it!

The kingdom is forever grateful for the Golden Flower that saved the Queen. As the flower grew from a drop of sunlight, the kingdom's emblem is a shining sun.

*Colorful petals decorate Rapunzel's hair*

One of Rapunzel's favorite parts of her birthday in the kingdom is when some children braid her hair with flowers.

*The kingdom rises above a beautiful, shimmering lake*

## Majestic Kingdom

The magnificent kingdom is rich in tradition and beauty. The King and Queen, Rapunzel's true parents, rule with generosity and kindness. Their prosperous subjects love them and share their hope that someday their lost princess will return.

*Like a kind guardian, the castle keeps watch over the town below*

*Large sailing boats and gondolas often travel on the calm waters of the lake*

# Birthday

Rapunzel has always loved her birthday. The floating lights made her feel really special. But this year her birthday is better than she could ever have imagined. As she explores the kingdom with Flynn, Pascal, and Max, her heart is filled with joy. Today she will be able to see the floating lights up close for the first time.

Rapunzel and Flynn release their own lanterns from a boat. Rapunzel feels she has made a great discovery in finding the kingdom and meeting the people outside her tower.

## True Love's Light

As they watch the floating lanterns glow overhead from their gondola, Rapunzel and Flynn realize that something even more magical has happened for them both. Love is beginning to blossom between them.

## Magic in the Air

As night falls, the King and Queen and their people release their lanterns to honor their lost princess. The lights glow against the dark sky. It is pure magic—and a dream come true for Rapunzel to see them up close.

Flynn is a changed man. He no longer cares about the crown—Rapunzel is all that matters. Back on shore, he sees the Stabbingtons and leaves Rapunzel to give the crown back to them. It's not important now. But the brothers know about Rapunzel's magic hair and now they want her instead!

The guards have finally caught their most wanted man. They feel victorious—but Flynn just wants to get back to Rapunzel.

## Revenge

Ever since Flynn ran out on them, the Stabbingtons have been hungry for revenge. Now they have him where they want him—tied to a boat with the crown tied to his hand. He is heading straight for the palace guards and prison!

## Mother was Right

Rapunzel thinks Flynn has left her. The brokenhearted girl flies into her mother's arms—just as the wicked woman planned.

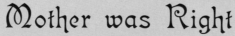

## Powerless in Prison

The Stabbingtons are imprisoned with Flynn. When they tell him they heard about Rapunzel's magic hair from Mother Gothel, Flynn realizes that Rapunzel is in trouble. He hates feeling helpless.

Flynn constantly ponders how to escape.

Flynn may be powerless to help Rapunzel but Maximus is not and he knows just what to do. He gallops to fetch the thugs who are happy to help.

## Jail Break

They might make an unlikely team, but Maximus, Flynn, and the pub thugs have one thing in common—they all love Rapunzel. With the thugs' help, Flynn catapults from the prison onto Max's back and races to rescue Rapunzel.

Back in the tower, Rapunzel finally realizes the truth: She is the lost princess! Soon after, Flynn arrives but Mother Gothel stabs him. As Flynn lies dying, Mother Gothel gives Rapunzel a choice—freedom or Flynn. Of course, Rapunzel chooses Flynn, but he cuts her magical hair before she can save him! Instantly, Rapunzel's hair loses its power and Mother Gothel turns to dust.

Rapunzel is free at last, but at the cost of Flynn's life. Brokenhearted, Rapunzel weeps and a single tear touches Flynn—he lives! The last bit of magic inside Rapunzel saved him. Finally, Rapunzel goes home to her true mother and father...

...And they can all live happily ever after.

# Acknowledgments

LONDON, NEW YORK, MELBOURNE,
MUNICH, AND DELHI

**Project Editor** Victoria Taylor
**Senior Designer** Guy Harvey
**Managing Editor** Catherine Saunders
**Art Director** Lisa Lanzarini
**Publishing Manager** Simon Beecroft
**Category Publisher** Alex Allan
**Production Editor** Siu Yin Chan
**Production Controller** Nick Seston

First American Edition, 2010
10 11 12 13 14 10 9 8 7 6 5 4 3 2 1
Published in the United States by DK Publishing
375 Hudson Street, New York, New York 10014

176205—09/10

A catalog record for this book is available from the
Library of Congress.

ISBN: 978-0-7566-6688-0

Color reproduction by Printing LTD
Printed and bound by Lake Book Manufacturing, Inc.

### Acknowledgments

The publisher would like to thank the following people:

Chelsea Nissenbaum, Deborah Boone, Lauren Kressel,
Leigh Anna MacFadden, Shiho Tilley, and Vickie Saxon at
Disney Publishing Worldwide; Katie Carter and Roy Conli
at Walt Disney Animation Studios; and Renato Lattanzi
at Disney Consumer Products; Daniel Peterson for
additional design work; Laura Gilbert and Lisa Stock
for editorial assistance.

Discover more at
www.dk.com